# ROSIE KNOWS

## A DOG'S LOOK AT LIFE

### ROSIE RUBIN

Balboa Press books may be ordered through booksellers or by contacting:

Balboa Press
A Division of Hay House
1663 Liberty Drive
Bloomington, IN 47403
www.balboapress.com.au
1 (877) 407-4847

ISBN: 978-1-5043-1572-2 (sc)
ISBN: 978-1-5043-1571-5 (e)

Print information available on the last page.

Balboa Press rev. date: 11/09/2018

BALBOA
PRESS
A DIVISION OF HAY HOUSE

# CONTENTS

# FROM MY KENNEL TO YOURS

OH!

*There* you are! Hello!

I am Rosie and I would like to shake paws with you.

This book contains quite a few words that I have never heard before but my owner Miss Polly says that words are a good way of sharing thoughts, so I will try this human way of sharing.

In our dogs world we don't use words because we have our special senses but I think it is pretty cool to share with you this way.

Of course the disadvantage of this communication is that we cannot sniff each other or share licks and growls, or even run and chase crows together which is what we dogs do naturally. It may take a little more time to tell you about me... even though a sniff would have saved us time!

I am a dog, an ordinary dog, the four paws, wet nose, and waggy tail variety.

I know that we dogs are in almost every country of the world, just like you humans.

I was born right here in Australia... Where do you come from?

I live in a small town called Tenterfield on the Northern Tablelands of New South Wales with my owner Miss Polly.

She is a kind lady who feeds me nice meaty bones, gives me a fresh bowl of water each morning and talks to me just like a human.

She does expect me to do a few things for her like sit, stay, not pull on my harness and come when she calls me,but I am happy to do all that *most of the time* because it is my way of being grateful to her for caring for me.

I have the occasional treat when we go shopping (I dream of it often!) and Miss Polly seems to know when I need a pat or an ear scratch.

She is gentle when she brushes my shiny coat especially around my eyes and nose and every week she will give me a bath (if she can catch me!)

The best treat of all is when we go to town.

I love riding in the car with the window down because there are so many wonderful smells... Cattle, Kangaroos, all the different types of Australian trees, blossoms, birds and rabbits... I *love* rabbits!

Yes, you guessed it, Miss Polly and I live on a farm outside of town with a lot of

grassy paddocks and fences with gates to keep animals off the road. It smells so wonderful as I have a super dog nose!

The farm is quite different to the place I lived before I met Miss Polly, which had a lot more cars and people, but I will tell you about that another time.

Right now I am bursting to tell you about all my adventures which are real... because remember I am a real dog!

I am so happy and excited to try this human way of sharing with you, my tail is wagging itself!

Is yours?

Oops, I forgot you don't have a tail.

I won't feel too sorry for you though and just accept That it is a difference that makes me, ME and you, YOU.

Although there are many differences between dogs and humans, some things are the same so I think we will get along fine.

Talk soon,

Rosie

# ❀ WEAR A SMILE; SHARE A SMILE! ❀

Hello again from Rosie!

Do you go to school?

So do I!

Miss Polly and I visit local schools where we meet with all the kids and some teachers too.

We visit classrooms and watch how you human pups learn stuff... which is a bit different from how we dogs learn, but it must work quite well because some of you humans are pretty smart.

I like it best when the school bell rings and everyone goes into the recess area to talk and laugh and run around. I especially love it when kids open their lunch boxes... so many delicious smells!

Of course Miss Polly is pretty strict about me not accepting food from students, but can I help it if a little scrap of yummy human food lands at my feet? Miss Polly does not see everything! He! He!

It seems to me that students like going to school but occasionally I see some sad faces, sitting alone and not enjoying it at all. I want to go over to them and wag my tail and look cute so that they will smile again.

I hear teachers talking about how they are trying to make school a place where everyone (including teachers) can enjoy each day. They do seem to have good ideas, but they also look so busy and rush around a fair bit too.

It seems to me that school is a place where young human kids come together to

learn important things like reading and stuff but also to hang out with friends, take care of each other, share and laugh.

I like listening to humans laughing... we dogs don't do that!

I am guessing that the learning continues after the bell rings and everyone goes to their home because in a dogs world that is where the most important learning of all happens.

We watch our parents and older dogs and learn how to bury bones and chase crows or sometimes if we are being too noisy and annoying we get a nip or growl from the older dogs.

We think of it as life learning and it keeps happening, even when we get older.

**We dogs have days that are good and some days that can be really difficult.**

I am guessing that it is the same for humans?

I once met a very angry Doberman and that **<u>was</u>** a bad day, my tail was definitely **<u>not</u>** wagging when he started to growl at me, and chased me with his big teeth.

I was a bit scared and ran as fast as I could back home where I met some of my family in the yard and they helped me find a bone that I had buried a week ago so I felt happy again.

That's how it goes in a dog's world.... We help each other and we prefer to be happy because feels better.

Of course it's difficult to be happy all the time (even my tail gets pretty tired!)

If you see someone looking sad and lonely at school why not share a smile or say "Hi " just to let them know someone cares.

Here's a poem I wrote for you and Miss Polly has translated my woofs into words that you can understand.

*"This tail is made for wagging …and that's just what I do*

*You have no tail my human friends…I feel sorry for you*

*But I can see you feel like me and want to share your Joy*

*So be a friend and Share a smile with  to every girl and boy.* (Including parents!)

Am I a Poet dog now?

Woof Woof!!

Rosie

# ❧ EXCUSE ME! ❧

Hello again friends

Woofs to you!

How have you been?

My tail is not wagging as much today as I got into trouble. Can I tell you about it?

I wasn't bad or anything, but I just got a bit excited and forgot my manners.

I ran after a moving car which made Miss Polly very annoyed as she was worried I would get hurt by those fast moving wheels.

She doesn't understand that those wheels were just wanting me to chase them and they were always just one bite away from me catching up.

This was very annoying and I admit that I was barking a lot!

Miss Polly said **"NO "**which is a word that always feels like a bite or a sharp needle.

When I was a pup I seemed to always be in trouble for chewing up shoes, digging holes in the yard or just barking at another dog as we drove through town.

**"NO"** was a word I learned to understand pretty quickly.

Even as a pup I knew that some things could be annoying to others, even though I didn't really know exactly why, but I did know that I was expected to stop doing it.

I worked out that to apologise is to admit that what I did was not acceptable and to recognise that it has caused hurt or disappointment to another.

I was just a pup and wanted so much to make everything right again.

I wanted pats and ear scratches and hear people say "Good dog"

I guess that sometimes there is nothing else to do to make things right, except to apologise.

Often a lick worked well because I was sooo cute!!

I have to say that it can be easy to get into the habit of beating yourself up and apologizing for everything... .that just makes you feel bad.

My friend Bindy is like that, always running off with her tail between her legs if she even hears a raised voice and she thinks that everything is her fault.

That's taking things too far! She is a dog like me and still learning how to behave.

I tell her "Be proud to be who you are even if you do make mistakes, nobody's perfect.

There are times when it does not seem fair that people do not say sorry to me when they tread on my paws, or forgot to fill my water bowl or use the garden hose to wash off all those great smells of cow manure I so carefully rolled in!

Miss Polly says I still have a lot to learn and I guess she is right.

I am like you, just growing up.

If this stuff happens to you and you find yourself in the position where an apology is the best choice, there is no replacement for the words: **"I'm sorry"**

If you have made a mistake or upset a friend or your family or your teacher, just say "I'm sorry" and mean it! I find it is the best way.

If someone apologizes to you, then thank them... 'ços you know it is not easy to say "Sorry".

I think it is a brave thing to do.

Once you let people know that you are sorry and will try not to offend them you will be friends again, chasing a ball together or sharing a smelly bone... or whatever you humans do!

Life is too short to miss out on having a good time with friends!

Big Licks,

Rosie

# 🐾 TIME FOR PAWS 🐾

Woofs to you! Rosie here.

I went for my usual run this morning, as we dogs do, and the grass was so cold on my paws, so I now can understand why you humans wear socks and shoes.

I was not thinking about my paws at the time though as I was on a mission.

Those pesky crows were all around the hen house stealing the grain and it is my special job to chase them away.

I love this job especially when I can show off my fastest running and bark loudly.

The exercise is great.

Sometimes I just run around for fun, or chase my tail, even run after rabbits if they pop their heads up. Rabbits are pretty fast you know and they often disappear down holes in the ground all of a sudden.

As for crows,well they don't play fair at all,they flap their wings and fly up into the trees and I see them laughing at me saying "Better luck next time Loser!"

It makes me so mad but I'll get them next time... so I will!

Exercise warms me up and I feel so good... like my whole body is revving like a car engine ready for action and my mind is clear and alert.

The sky looks bluer and the trees greener and the earth seems to vibrate under my paws, but that could be my imagination I guess.

I am thinking humans also like exercise as I see them running and riding bicycles in town and some are pretty fit, just like we dogs!

What I don't understand is why some people spend a long time staring at a little screen in their hands and talking to it for such a long time.

When Miss Polly talks to that gadget I feel like I don't exist. I want to bark and play because there are more fun things to do than looking at screens.

She is not impressed at all when I make whining noises and she tells me to use my manners and **wait!**

I try to do something else but sometimes it's no fun alone.

Once when I was a pup I was so bored that I chewed through a plastic cable... oh! oh! did I get into big trouble and Miss Polly did not pat me for hours!

I have now found a way that works better and does not get me into trouble. It is something an old dog taught me and I am not sure what you call it but it is a way of keeping my thoughts on one thing and not allowing my mind to wander.

I just curl up somewhere quiet and close my eyes, which looks like I am sleeping, but I am really just listening to my breathing and being aware of everything around me but not **<u>doing</u>** anything.

I hear the sounds of the crows but I don't need to chase them, I feel the breeze

on my super sensitive nose, just know it is there. Sometimes I can even hear my belly making rumbly sounds.

I just seem to have a mind full of now... I don't think of yesterday or tomorrow and I dont do anything at all except just BE in the moment.

I feel really calm and time seems to disappear.

Before I know it Miss Polly has finished talking to the screen and is picking up the tennis ball... And you know what that means?

I seem to have heaps of energy and can chase that ball for longer than ever!

A fully charged up doggy machine!

I expect you know all this but I am still learning, after all I am just a dog!

Talk soon,

Rosie

# 🐾 MINDFULNESS 🐾

Hello again from Rosie!

Just thought I would check in with you all... in between naps!

Dogs get tired like humans especially on dull and cloudy days that seem to make us want to sleep more. We dogs understand this very well as we know that body energy rhythms change with the seasons and I am guessing it is the same for humans.

I have to say that I have noticed that humans seem to expect more from their body than we dogs,a kind of "push through the tiredness "attitude, which does not seem to work too well. Again it seems we dogs are a bit smarter.

When we are tired we just curl up somewhere quietly and have a nap.

Sometimes a quick nap and sometimes a long one...but when we wake up we feel fully recharged and ready to chase rabbits and crows,

I know it is not as easy for humans, you have places to be and things to do that do not allow you to have a quick nap whenever you wish.

I have been watching Miss Polly and she seems to have a way of recharging her energy.

I am sure she will not mind if I share it with you.

Of course she does not stay up too late or drink lots of coffee or canned drinks before bed.

That's sensible.

She has this way of "unplugging" from the world every now and again.

She just sits in silence, quite still and does not appear to "do" anything except breathe.

She calls it Mindfulness Meditation.

I rather like it too even though I fall asleep most times.

I guess that this Mindfulness has much the same effect as my mini-naps, so perhaps humans are almost as smart as dogs after all!!

What seems to get in the way of this silence with some humans I see is a "ping" or "brrr-ing" from those screen devices.

They loudly demand that you give all your attention right NOW! It must be a very important gadget!

If I am resting and I hear the brrr-ing I feel like chewing that little screen into small pieces with my big doggy teeth, but Miss Polly says that there is a switch that can silence it or turn it off completely...too easy!! Why didn't I think of that??

Unplugging from those devices is not easy but like Miss Polly says it is all about deciding what is more important. As a smart dog I know the answer... do you?

Sometimes not being available to others is more helpful in saving our own energy. Perhaps call them back later...or not!

We have a doggy saying:

"You can't share from an empty doggy bowl"

Can I share the best of me if I am tired, cranky and out of energy.

Noooo!

Makes sense eh?

I will talk again about this mindfulness.

I need to watch Miss Polly for a while to work it out and get back to you!

Nice to chat but I really need to have another nap!

Talk later,

Rosie

Woof Woof

# 🐾 DOING THE BEST I CAN 🐾

Hello my human friends.

Thanks for all your letters to me..I am so pleased that you like my stories.

I like to hear that you think I am cute and yes Mary, I think I could become a cheer leader dog one day!! Great idea!

Just a quick update on my studies... you know I am on a doggy course to become a Therapy dog.

Well let me tell you it is not as easy as I thought and sometimes I wish I had never started it.

I am sharing this with you this because some school students have told me that they find studies difficult too.

Like them I am really trying my best, well mostly, which makes me feel good, even though at times I think Miss Polly expects more from me.

I expect you know what I mean.

I know she wants me to succeed and has faith in me as she really believes I am quite a talented dog.

Hmm! Could she be right? I feel quite proud of her belief in me and I believe in me too!

Doing the best I can is all I can do and Yes... My best is often not as good as Charlie's best.

You remember Charlie, the big black Labrador in town who is good at everything without even seeming to try!!

He even wears his harness willingly!!

I feel limited in what I can achieve when I look at Charlie... but one thing I can do is my best.

I am in charge of that, not Charlie!

What he finds easy I find difficult, that's true, but he _is_ a Labrador!

He is naturally better at swimming in the creek and can chew bigger bones and smart stuff like that, but when it comes to mustering sheep or chasing down a rabbit... I leave him waaaay behind!

Now I am guessing it is much the same for you human kids as you have your own special talents and you how important it is to do your best, at least that is under your control!

Like me you will know the difference between saying "I am doing my best" and really _meaning_ it.

I am still not sure how Miss Polly knows when I am just saying it.

I do the whole "sad eyes and pleading look" act but she still knows!

Humans have a special sense I think!

All I know is that I feel great when I know I am really doing my best and I feel even better when Miss Polly knows it too.

My tail seems to wag itself!

I am slowly working towards my finals when I hope to graduate as a proper school therapy dog. That will be a tail wagging day to remember!

Thanks for listening... I really find it helps to share my stuff with you.

I gotta get back to my studies now.

I am really looking forward to my exams and I really will do MY best!!

Licks and Woofs

Rosie

# GRR! BUT JUST DO IT

Woofs to you from Rosie!

I am sniffing the air and I think the weather is changing here in my part of the world.

The sky has been cloudier for some time now and the air cooler. In fact I have noticed that my lovely black coat has become thicker and glossier over the last few months and warmer too.

The days have been quite short recently and sometimes when I have my bowl of dog food the sun has already gone down and the moon is appearing.

We dogs have a sense when things are changing and I think that warmer weather and longer days are coming.

Miss Polly was driving me in the car yesterday and I had my head out of the window sniffing the air. I noticed that the trees are starting to blossom and my super sensitive nose was a bit itchy.

The old leaves are mulching into the ground and there seem to be more rabbits hopping about the paddocks. People seem to be friendlier and I am seeing a few more wagging tails with my doggy friends'

I even saw a great big rainbow at the farm gate.

Is it true there is a big bone at the end of the rainbow?

There is still a bit of a chill on my paws when I chase the crows across the grass in the morning, but I am hoping that the grass will get greener soon.

Miss Polly says we need more rain to make everything greener but I do not like rain as it reminds me of when I have a bath! Grr!

Miss Polly likes to bring out the doggy tub every week and rub me all over with a very clean smelling shampoo.

I try to stand still so that I don't get it in my eyes but it takes a lot of self discipline which is something I am still trying to learn.

I must say I do like people telling me I am a good looking dog and complimenting me on my fine sweet smelling glossy coat, so I guess it is worth it.

It seems we all have to do things that we don't like, but it usually ends up being the easiest way.

We don't have to like it but we just do it because the reward is more important.

I remember when Miss Polly took me to the Vet surgery and I had my teeth cleaned.

Oh! I never want to go there again. Makes my teeth sore just to think about it, but like Miss Polly says it is better to get things checked before they become a problem.

She is usually right.

Meanwhile I will not worry about teeth cleaning or doggy baths because I want to stay in this happy moment.

Like Miss Polly says, there's no point in thinking about yesterday because it is gone, and tomorrow is not here yet!

That makes sense to me.

So my friends I am away down the paddock to enjoy myself because i notices some cow manure down by the farm gate and it will smell so much better than doggy shampoo! Shhh! Don't tell Miss Polly!

Perhaps it is because the seasons are changing that I feel as happy as a circus dog!!

Woofs and Licks

Rosie

# 🐾 RIDE THAT WAVE! 🐾

Hello again Rosie here!

Have you ever been on holidays to the beach?

I just did that recently for the very first time in my doggy life and I simply must tell you about it!!

Of course you know that I live on a farm up on the tablelands in Australia and there is no ocean up here, in fact we are hundreds of metres above sea level.

Australia is a great big continent entirely surrounded by ocean so I was so excited when Miss Polly said we were going to the Gold Coast which is several hours drive from here.

I was not prepared for what I saw.

The first thing I noticed was that there were a lot more people at the coast, some very tall apartment buildings and a strange salty smell in the air.

Miss Polly drove to a sandy place and she parked the car because we had to walk a way to get to this ocean.

As we walked I noticed that the ground was not like the grass at home, but kind of gritty and it got in between my toes.

It was then I saw the ocean... oh! My! *"What is this?"* I thought to myself, it looks like lots of space to run but it is moving and it is **wet!**

I tried to drink it but it was too salty and the sand was so soggy underneath that I felt my paws sinking.

Dogs are naturally curious animals and I was absolutely fascinated by this scene as if my eyes had opened into a different world.

I watched some human kids having fun playing in this ocean and wanted to go and join them, but when I did it was like having a bath and all of a sudden I found myself with no paws!!

I was running but not touching the ground and the salty water got in my eyes and up my nose!

It was so scary and I became a little panicky! It seemed to me that this ocean was huge and seemed to stretch forever!

I wondered how a dog could run in that or how even humans could!

I got back to the shore and found my paws again. I shook my wet coat all over Miss Polly who was not impressed but laughed at me and told me it was ok.

I sat and watched this ocean for a while from the safety of the soft dry sand and saw some young humans on flat boards. They were paddling almost out of sight then jumping on their board and riding back on the top of a wave.

It looked difficult but even when they fell off the board they did it again. I thought that it was a very brave thing to do because this ocean seemed to be changeable and the wind made the waves choppy.

*"Why would anyone do that?"* I thought. I was very puzzled.

I am back home on the farm now and I think about that holiday.

I was so scared in the ocean because I felt out of control, with the waves splashing my face and eyes and I was unable to touch solid ground.

I thought too about those board riders who seemed to enjoy it so much.

I think Miss Polly would say something like:

*"You can't stop the waves but you can learn to ride them"*

That's the way Miss Polly talks when she helps students with their problems at school when they get anxious and fearful. I think I get what she means now.

When scary things happen and life seems hard to handle (like the ocean) there is a way to deal with it by focusing on the helpful waves that get you to the shore instead of looking at the whole ocean which seems impossible to manage!

I wish I could have remembered that when I was in that deep ocean getting almost drowned!!

I guess that is why we dogs are not water animals.

Naturally you humans know about this stuff already!

But I am just a dog!

Now... Where did I bury that nice bone last week?

It should be really smelly and delicious by now!!

Woofs

Rosie

# 🐾 NOW ROSIE KNOWS 🐾

Hello again.

*"Miss Polly had a doggy who was sick, sick, sick!"*

That was ME a few days ago!!!

I had something happening in my body that was not good...and I was "sick as a dog"!

Now I know why people use that phrase because a dog being sick is **not** pretty.

I was tired, stressed and definitely unhappy.

I even had to get a needle at the Vet!

That made me even crankier.

Who sticks needles into someone to make them better???

Of course I know now that without that needle I could have been a whole lot worse.

Miss Polly says that sometimes we just have to look at the bigger picture... but that's not easy when you feel so sick!

You may have felt this way. Can you remember?

My head hurt, my nose was hot and dry and my legs just did not want to run, even after those pesky crows!

I was really irritable and just wanted to roll up and hide from the world.

In fact, I even growled, "leave me alone" at Miss Polly when she tried to get me to have a drink from my bowl. I feel sorry about that.

Today my tail is wagging again but being sick made me realize that this may be why some other dogs or even humans can appear so unfriendly and cranky... could they feel the way I did?

Missy (my Chihuahua city dog friend) was sick with her cut paw pads some time ago and it hurt her to walk.

I think that is why she growled and showed me her needle sharp teeth when I wanted to play with her. I was pretty annoyed at the time and my feelings were hurt. I was confused. What had I done?

I refused to share my bones with her for ages after that!

I realize now that she was just feeling unwell and it was nothing to do with me at all! If I had Missy's paws that day I would have understood and shared my bones with her to show I cared. I will do that next time

Polly says that is called **Compassion** and it seems to me that this word means being a bit more understanding and not judging people.

I am sure that kind of thing happens with humans too.

Do you ever feel like someone is being mean to you for no reason?

It might help to remember how you felt when you were sick and how difficult it was to be polite...or even talk.

Just smile and ask'

"RU Ok" and wag your tail!

Oops. I forgot... You don't have a tail do you?

Bye for now!!

Rosie

# AND THEY CALL IT... PUPPY LOVE

My friends say that I am looking good these days!

My eyes are brighter, I look slimmer and my coat is glossier than it has ever been!

I think I am in LOVE!

Can I tell you about it?

His name is Nevada and he is GORGEOUS!

He is a caramel creamy coloured Labrador, very handsome with big brown eyes and a deep husky bark that is like thunder in the hills.

He is strong and super smart and all my friends say he likes me too.

Our wet noses met through the fence last week and my heart was beating so fast that I felt as though I had been chasing rabbits for an hour. As soon as our eyes met we both knew this was everlasting love.

He was excited too and chased his tail for quite some time until he got dizzy and started to stagger about as though his legs were made of jelly! We both laughed!

Nevada belongs to a vision impaired man called Mike and they have both had very special training.

I am sure Nevada was top of his doggy class.

Polly walks me past his fence often now on her way to school and she lets us play for a minute and we make doggy noises. It is the highlight of my day!

I even **dream** of him!

I feel wonderful when I see him and I think this must be doggy heaven.

When I am not with Nevada I get these thoughts which are not so good.

I wonder if I am pretty enough and I secretly worry that he will find another dog more attractive and forget about me.

I have never felt these feelings before and I must say they are not comfortable.

Nevada could see I was worried and so I told him about it.

I said that I just wanted to be the fastest, cleverest, prettiest dog in town just to please him but I was worried that he would think I was not good enough

He just smiled and licked my face and then told me (in doggy talk)

"I like you because you are YOU!"

"You don't need to change or try to be anything for me."

"Just be exactly who you are right now."

He also told me that we have all the time in the world to just enjoy being

together and learning more about each other because that is how a trusting relationship develops.

I wanted to lick him all over because I felt so happy but Miss Polly could hear the school bell ringing which meant we would be late for school assembly, so we hurried away.

I could see him wagging his tail and running up and down the fence as we turned the corner into School Road.

My feet seemed to be walking on clouds and my heart was like a balloon bouncing inside my chest.

I spent all that morning thinking about him when I should have been concentrating on my work with Miss Polly.

Is this what they call Puppy Love?

Please tell me. I am new to this.

Rosie

Printed in the United States
By Bookmasters